Ripley's **Believe It or Not!** ®

Mind Teasers

GETTING THERE

Published by
Capstone Press, Inc.
Mankato, Minnesota USA

1

CIP
LIBRARY OF CONGRESS CATALOGING IN PUBLICATION DATA

Getting there.
        p. cm. -- (Ripley's believe it or not! mind teasers)
        Summary: Presents surprising facts about bicycles, boats, cars, and other forms of transportation.

        ISBN 1-56065-067-2:
        1.   Transportation--Miscellanea--Juvenile   literature.   [1.
Transportation--Miscellanea. 2. Curiosities and wonders.]
I. Series
TA1149.G48   1991
629.04--dc20   91-19899
                                     CIP
                                     AC

Color Illustrations by Carol J. Stott

This edition published by Capstone Press, Inc., Box 669, Mankato, MN 56001. Printed in the United States of America.

CAPSTONE PRESS
Box 669, Mankato, MN 56001

Ripley's — Believe It or Not!®

CONTENTS

Introduction   5

Airplanes   7

Bicycles and Motorcycles   11

Cars and Trucks   17

Ships and Boats   26

Trains   31

Unusual Ways of Getting There   35

Believe It or Not!   42

4

Introduction

The man that created Ripley's Believe It or Not! was Robert L. Ripley. Ripley grew up in Santa Rosa, California. His two main interests throughout his youth were drawing and sports. By the time he was 25, Ripley was working in New York for the Globe as a sports illustrator.

One day, when Ripley needed to fill space in the newspaper, he found a scrapbook with unusual achievements in sports in his files. He drew illustrations for 9 of these and titled the art "Champs and Chumps." Ripley's editor retitled the work "Believe It or Not!" This was published on December 19, 1918. The column was so popular that "Believe It or Not!" was set up as a regular weekly column. It was not long before it was a daily cartoon.

In 1929, Ripley was one of the top cartoonists in the country. His Believe It or Not! feature was one of the hottest columns in the newspaper. He had also published a book and was now anxious to search for new material. For the next few years he traveled thousands of miles. He visited 198 different countries. At first he returned with many souvenirs of personal interest. Soon, he started returning with huge crates of curiosities. His friends encouraged him to put his treasures on public display.

Ripley's first display was in 1933 at Chicago's Century of Progress Exposition. In two seasons 2,470,739 people lined up to see his incredible treasures. Now Ripley was in demand on the lecture circuit. Next came movies, a top-rated radio show, more books and finally television. By 1940, Ripley had three "Odditoriums" running simultaneously - one at the Golden Gate International Exposition in San Francisco, California; one at the World's Fair at Flushing Meadows, New York; and another on Broadway in New York City. A number of trailer shows toured the country. Ripley was very famous by the time of his death in 1949.

The information included in this special Mind Teaser Edition is from original Ripley's Believe It or Not! amazing archives of cartoons.

Ripley's Believe It or Not!®
Airplanes

"DOUBLE TAKE"
AMERICAN *CRAIG HOSKING* FLIES A PLANE THAT CAN TAKE OFF AND LAND *UPSIDE DOWN!*

EPPO NUMAN OF THE NETHERLANDS *WAS THE FIRST PERSON TO SUCCESSFULLY FLY A SINGLE-SEAT ULTRALIGHT ACROSS THE ATLANTIC OCEAN!*

TIM LANCASTER, A BRITISH AIRWAYS PILOT FLYING A JET-LINER AT 20,000 FT., WAS SAVED FROM BEING SUCKED THROUGH THE GLASS OF A BROKEN WINDSHIELD BY CREW MEMBERS WHO HELD *HIS ANKLES!*

IN THE 1920s, TWO DAREDEVIL FLYERS PLAYED TENNIS ON THE WING OF AN AIRPLANE *IN FLIGHT!*

IN 1938, MILLIONAIRE **HOWARD HUGHES** SET A ROUND-THE-WORLD SPEED RECORD FLYING A PLANE THAT WAS **FILLED WITH PING-PONG BALLS** IN CASE HE CRASHED OVER WATER!

American pilot *Hank Dempsey* fell out of an airplane flying at 2,500 ft. And hung for 20 min. from the plane's stairs until the copilot safely landed the aircraft!

Scientists in Greenland, using ground-penetrating radar, discovered a squadron of World War II planes buried under 260 feet of ice and snow! *The planes had been missing for 47 years!*

9

PAUL MOLLER, AN ENGINEER IN DAVIS, CA., DESIGNS AND BUILDS *FULL-SIZE FLYING SAUCERS* THAT CAN *HOVER 40 FEET ABOVE THE GROUND!*

A U.S. JET PILOT CAN BE TRAINED IN 13 *MONTHS*, BUT IT TAKES 15 *MONTHS* FOR A BANDMASTER TO TRAIN AT THE PENTAGONS SCHOOL OF MUSIC!

ELEVEN-YEAR-OLD TONY ALIENGENA of San Juan Capistrano, Ca., IS THE *YOUNGEST PILOT TO FLY AROUND THE WORLD!* THE FIFTH-GRADER FLEW 17,000 MILES IN 7 WEEKS!

Ripley's — Believe It or Not!®

Bicycles and Motorcycles

BRITISH CYCLIST *REG HARRIS,* WHO SURVIVED BEING BLOWN UP IN A TANK DURING WWII AND BREAKING HIS NECK IN A CAR ACCIDENT, *WENT ON TO WIN FOUR WORLD RACING TITLES!*

BELIEVE IT OR NOT! IN 1928, LEON VANDERSTUYFT, A BELGIAN CYCLIST, PEDALED 76 MI. AND 504 YDS. *IN ONE HOUR* — A RECORD THAT HAS BEEN UNMATCHED FOR MORE THAN 60 YEARS!

STEVE ROBERTS OF COLUMBUS, OHIO, HAS TRAVELED 20,000 MILES ON A HIGH-TECH BICYCLE THAT FEATURES 36 GEARS, 5 COMPUTERS AND A TELEVISION.

FRED HILLIARD, a Wyoming school teacher, and his DOG WOLSOY HAVE SPENT THE LAST 7 YEARS TRAVELING TOGETHER ACROSS 27 STATES AND THROUGH WESTERN CANADA — ON A MOTORCYCLE!

"WORLD'S SMALLEST UNICYCLE" CHARLIE CHARLES, A TRICK RIDER PEDALS A UNICYCLE THAT MEASURES ONLY 5 3/4 INCHES IN HEIGHT.!

AMERICAN CYCLIST GREG LEMOND WON THE 1989, 23-DAY, 2000-MILE LONG *Tour de France* BICYCLE RACE DESPITE *40 SHOTGUN PELLETS* LEFT IN HIS BODY FROM A 1987 HUNTING ACCIDENT!

IN 1990, *KEVIN FOSTER* OF CALIF. RODE **3,700 MILES** ALONG THE GREAT WALL OF CHINA— *ON A BICYCLE!*

IN 1977, 8-YEAR-OLD MATTHEW HULLFISH RODE A BICYCLE **3,606 MILES** FROM SAN FRANCISCO, CA, TO ATLANTIC CITY, NJ!

MECHANIC **DAVE MOORE** OF ROSEMEAD, CA, BUILT AN 8FT. HIGH METAL MONOCYCLE *FROM DESIGNS DRAWN 500 YEARS AGO BY LEONARDO DA VINCI!*

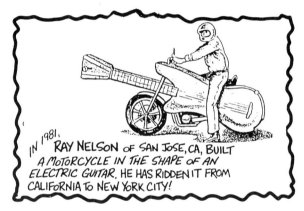

IN 1981, **RAY NELSON** OF SAN JOSE, CA, BUILT A MOTORCYCLE IN THE SHAPE OF AN ELECTRIC GUITAR. HE HAS RIDDEN IT FROM CALIFORNIA TO NEW YORK CITY!

ALAN FREEMAN, A RETIRED BRITISH ENGINEER, INVENTED A *SOLAR BICYCLE* THAT GATHERS ENERGY FROM A SOLAR PANEL INSTALLED ON THE HANDLEBARS! IT CAN GO FOR 30 MILES AND REACH A SPEED OF 15 MPH!

GENNAI YANAGISAWA OF JAPAN INVENTED A *MOTORIZED BICYCLE*, PROPELLED BY A 17-LB. FAN, *THAT CAN REACH A SPEED OF 60 MPH.!*

ON APRIL 1987, SHINJI KAZAMA OF TOKYO, JAPAN, BECAME THE FIRST MAN TO RIDE A MOTORCYCLE TO THE *NORTH POLE*—COVERING 770 KM IN 44 DAYS.!

IN 1967, STEVE McPEAK OF TACOMA, WASH., *RODE A 4-STORY-HIGH UNICYCLE FOR 100 FT.!*

IN 1884, THOMAS STEVENS, AN ENGLISH JOURNALIST, RODE AROUND THE WORLD ON A *10 FT-HIGH* PENNY-FARTHING BICYCLE!

PATENT# 190,644, A PATENT FOR A VELOCIPEDE WITH A CARRIAGE AND A HOLLOW FRONT WHEEL THAT IS POWERED BY 2 RUNNING DOGS, WAS FILED AT THE U.S. PATENT OFFICE BY H.C. MEY OF BUFFALO, N.Y.!

EDITH WILSON, THE WIFE OF U.S. PRESIDENT *WOODROW WILSON* OFTEN RODE A *BICYCLE IN THE CORRIDORS OF THE WHITEHOUSE!*

Cars and Trucks

MABEL YEE OF EMERYVILLE, CALIF., DESIGNS PRODUCTS FOR COMMUTERS INCLUDING A *MASSAGING CAR SEAT* AND A *PORTABLE CAR FRIDGE AND STOVE!*

AUTOMAKER *HENRY FORD* ONCE CREATED A SUIT, A HAT AND PARTS OF A *CAR* — INCLUDING *LICENSE PLATES, WINDOW RIMS AND GAS PEDALS* — OUT OF **SOYBEANS!**

IN 1990, 170 VINTAGE CARS TOOK PART IN A *56-DAY*, *9800-MILE RACE* FROM *LONDON TO BEIJING, CHINA!*

GEORGE GIBSON OF
HAY RIVER, NORTHWEST
TERRITORY, WON A
NEW PICKUP TRUCK
BY FINDING THE TRUCK'S
KEY FROM 140 OTHERS
*WHILE SWIMMING IN A
POOL OF LIME GREEN
JELLO!*

LIVO di MARCHI OF VENICE, ITALY, BUILT A 3,300-LB.
WOODEN SCALE MODEL OF A 1930 JAGUAR CAR, POWERED
BY A 20 *HORSEPOWER
ENGINE TO SAIL THE
CITY'S CANALS!*

CARHENGE— JAMES REINDERS OF ALLIANCE, NE, BUILT A MONUMENT USING DOZENS OF **HALF-BURIED OLD CARS** SET IN A PATTERN *THAT RESEMBLES ENGLAND'S STONEHENGE!*

REG POLLARD OF MANCHESTER, ENGLAND, BUILT A 13-FT.-LONG REPLICA OF A 1907 "SILVER GHOST" ROLLS ROYCE USING 63 PINTS OF GLUE AND 1,016,711 *MATCHSTICKS.*

A SCULPTURE OF A GIANT BLOCK OF CONCRETE WITH CARS *EMBEDDED* IN ITS SURFACE IS USED **AS A ROAD MARKER** NEAR THE CITY OF JIDDAH, SAUDI ARABIA!

BEFORE THE FORD FAMILY NAMED THE EDSEL AFTER HENRY FORD'S SON, *THEY CONSIDERED 16,000 OTHER NAMES,* INCLUDING: "INTELLIGENT BULLET" "UTOPIAN TURTLETOP" AND "MONGOOSE CIVIQUE"!

BUY A *NEW* UTOPIAN TURTLETOP!

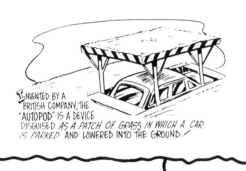

INVENTED BY A BRITISH COMPANY, THE "AUTOPOD" IS A DEVICE DISGUISED *AS A PATCH OF GRASS IN WHICH A CAR IS PARKED* AND LOWERED INTO THE GROUND.

IN 1972, ROBERT LAMAR OF HOUSTON, TEXAS, PATENTED A DESIGN FOR A TRUCK THAT WOULD AUTOMATICALLY THROW NEWSPAPERS ONTO SUBSCRIBERS' LAWNS.

from an old print.

AN **AUTOMOBILE** INVENTED IN PARIS, FRANCE, IN THE 18th CENTURY, NEEDED SO MUCH FUEL TO RUN ITS STEAM ENGINE THAT BAGS OF SOFT COAL **ALWAYS HAD TO BE LEFT ALONG ITS CHOSEN ROUTE**

IN 1930 JAMES HARGIS AND CHARLES CREIGHTON OF ST. LOUIS, MO, DROVE FROM NEW YORK CITY TO LOS ANGELES AND BACK— *IN REVERSE!*

LOS ANGELES

IN 1928, RACECAR DRIVER *FRANK LOCKHART* LOST CONTROL DRIVING AT A SPEED OF 225 MPH IN DAYTONA BEACH, FLA., YET SURVIVED THE CRASH THAT THREW HIS CAR 100 YARDS OUT TO SEA.!

Patent # 1,744,727
A DESIGN FOR A CAR MEGAPHONE FOR WARNING PEDESTRIANS WAS FILED AT THE U.S. PATENT OFFICE IN 1930!

JAMES McKINNIS AND JOHN TWEDDLE OF SAN ANTONIO, TX, SET A RECORD FOR MILEAGE ON A RENTED CAR WITH A WEEK'S FREE MILEAGE BY DRIVING FROM SAN ANTONIO TO LOS ANGELES, TO NEW YORK CITY, AND BACK AGAIN IN 7 DAYS!

NEW YORK 3000 MILES

Rent-a-Car

IN 1990, AMERICAN JAY OHRBERG DESIGNED AND BUILT A FERRARI SPORTS CAR THAT HAS 8 AXLES, 8 SEATS AND IS 9 *METERS LONG!*

IN 1983, HONDA DESIGNED AND BUILT A CAR THAT COULD DIVIDE INTO **TWO** AND HAD TWO SEPARATE ENGINES AND TWO STEERING WHEELS!

A COMPANY IN CALIF HAS DEVELOPED *"TRAVELPILOT"* A NAVIGATION SYSTEM THAT DISPLAYS MAPS OF CONGESTED TRAFFIC AREAS IN A COMPUTER SCREEN *MOUNTED ON CAR DASHBOARDS!*

BELIEVE IT OR NOT! THERE IS A 25-FT-HIGH PYRAMID OF HUBCAPS ON A HIGHWAY NEAR ATLANTIC CITY, N.J.!

BOB PRENOSIL OF CEDAR RAPIDS, MICH., REPORTED HIS 1937 FORD TUDOR STOLEN IN 1961, AND FOUND IT AT A SWAP MEET **29 YEARS LATER!**

IN 1927, FRANK ELLIOT AND GEORGE A. SCOTT OF NOVA SCOTIA, CANADA, TOOK A 4,759-MILE TRIP IN A MODEL T – BY PERSUADING *168 DIFFERENT MOTORISTS TO TOW THEIR CAR.*

DICK KEMP OF HILLSBORO, N.H., HAS A COLLECTION OF 85 MACK TRUCKS!

LEO GLADENSDAHL OF PRINCE GEORGE, B.C., DESIGNED AND BUILT *A 1,650 kg PLYWOOD CAR* WITH INVERTED DOG DISHES FOR HEADLIGHT RIMS AND A COMPUTER THAT MEASURES FUEL CONSUMPTION!

A VAN OWNED BY GEORGE D. KING OF POMPANO BEACH, FLA., IS DECORATED WITH **48,773 PENNIES!**

Ships and Boats

DURING **WORLD WAR II**, GEOFFREY PYKE OF ENGLAND WORKED AS A MILITARY ADVISOR AND MADE DESIGNS FOR AN **UNSINKABLE BATTLE-SHIP MADE FROM A MIXTURE OF ICE AND WOOD PULP!**

IN THE 1850s, THE JOINTED SHIP CO. OF LONDON, ENGLAND, BUILT A COAL VESSEL CALLED THE "CONNECTOR" WITH 3 *HINGED SECTIONS* THAT ROLLED WITH THE HIGH WAVES!

IN THE 17TH CENTURY, *CORNELIUS VAN DREBBEL* OF THE NETHERLANDS CROSSED LONDON'S THAMES RIVER *IN A SUBMARINE* MADE OF LEATHER AND *POWERED BY OARS!*

"BLUE NOVA" A 16.5-METER YACHT DESIGNED BY *JOHN WALKER* OF DEVONPORT, ENGLAND, *IS POWERED BY COMPUTER-CONTROLLED VERTICAL WINGS* INSTEAD OF SAILS!

DON PRICE of Santa Rosa, California, DESIGNED AND BUILT AN 18-FOOT MOTORBOAT *IN THE SHAPE OF A GUITAR!*

IN 1903, A FISHING BOAT OFF THE COAST OF NORMANDY SAILED FOR TWO DAYS *THROUGH A "BLIZZARD" OF WHITE BUTTERFLIES!*

IN MARCH, 1990, LESTER MORENO PEREZ ESCAPED CUBA BY WINDSURFING 60 MILES IN 16 HOURS ON A SAILBOARD *THROUGH THE FLORIDA STRAITS!*

JEREMY HIRST OF YORKSHIRE, ENGLAND, TRAVELED THE COUNTRYSIDE *IN A SAILBOAT* MOUNTED ON WHEELS, *WEARING A HAT THAT HAD A 9-FT. BRIM!*

THE KRONAN, A 17TH CENTURY WARSHIP, WAS THE **LARGEST VESSEL** IN THE SWEDISH NAVY AT 200 FEET AND 2350 TONS. IT TOOK 7 YEARS TO BUILD — *BUT WAS DESTROYED IN UNDER 1 MINUTE!*

IN 1824, A CANADIAN ENTREPRENEUR NAMED *MacPHERSON* BUILT A 3,700-TON WOODEN SHIP *MADE WITH REMOVABLE PEGS SO IT COULD BE EASILY DISMANTLED!*

CUNARD LINE, OWNERS OF THE QUEEN ELIZABETH II, HAVE STARTED A SPECIAL SERVICE THAT ALLOWS *NEXT-OF-KIN TO BOOK PASSAGE FOR A DECEASED PERSON WHO WISHES TO BE BURIED AT SEA!*

FOR $20,600 EACH, TOURISTS CAN TAKE A LUXURY CRUISE ON THE WORLD'S LARGEST **ICE-BREAKER**. THE TOUR INCLUDES A BARBEQUE DINNER AT THE *NORTH POLE!*

Ripley's—Believe It or Not!® Trains

RAILROAD CARS WERE USED AS *PUBLIC SCHOOLS* IN PARTS OF NORTHERN ONTARIO *FROM 1925-1964.*

PUBLIC SCHOOL

IN 1851 A PASSENGER TRAIN COLLIDED WITH A SCHOONER ON THE HUDSON RIVER *AFTER HEAVY FOG CAUSED THE SHIP TO BE GROUNDED!*

A CONSTRUCTION CREW TUNNELING INTO *NEW YORK'S FIRST SUBWAY* FOUND A 120-FT. *WAITING ROOM* WITH PAINTINGS, A FOUNTAIN AND A GRAND PIANO!

SARA GILLIES, AGE 9 MONTHS, OF PERTH, AUSTRALIA, SURVIVED INSIDE HER BABY CARRIAGE AFTER AN ACCIDENT IN WHICH THE CARRIAGE WAS HIT AND DRAGGED UNDER AN ONCOMING TRAIN!

IN 1989 A NEW HIGH-SPEED TRAIN DESIGNED AND BUILT IN FRANCE SET A NEW WORLD RECORD FOR *RAIL SPEED* OF 289 MPH.!

"THE SNOOZER"

DAN JAGDAT OF TORONTO, CANADA, INVENTED A *NOSE-SHAPED PILLOW* THAT STICKS TO WINDOWS FOR TRAVELERS AND COMMUTERS.!

N&L.R.R.

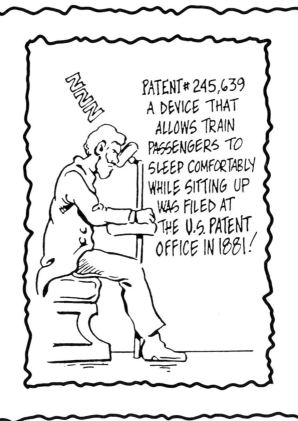

PATENT # 245,639 A DEVICE THAT ALLOWS TRAIN PASSENGERS TO SLEEP COMFORTABLY WHILE SITTING UP WAS FILED AT THE U.S. PATENT OFFICE IN 1881!

HENRY HAYES OF DENVER, COLO., DESIGNED AND PATENTED A STREETCAR TO BE POWERED BY A MECHANICAL HORSE, WITH HEADLIGHTS IN ITS EYES, ON A TREADMILL!

Ripley's — Believe It or Not!®
Unusual Ways of
Getting There

IN 1987, MICHAEL DIXON OF DANVILLE, IL, TRAVELED *100 MILES FROM HIS HOME* TO PERU, OH — WHILE **SLEEPWALKING!**

IN 1809, *CAPTAIN ALLARDYCE BARCLAY OF URY, SCOTLAND, IN A BET TO WIN $500,000, WALKED 1,000 MILES IN UNDER 1,000 HOURS!*

PARACHUTIST *MICHAEL LOEB* GOT TANGLED DURING A JUMP AND SPENT 20 MINUTES *DANGLING 1000 FT. ABOVE THE GROUND FROM A PLANE, TRAVELING 150 MPH!*

IN 1982, LARRY WALTERS OF LOS ANGELES, CALIF., *FLEW IN A LAWN CHAIR HELD UP BY 24 HELIUM-FILLED BALLOONS* TO A HEIGHT OF **3 MILES!**

PATENT # 363,037
IN 1887, CHARLES WULFF OF PARIS PATENTED A BALLOON USING EAGLES, VULTURES AND CONDORS FOR POWER AND STEERING.

LAURENT BOQUET, A FRENCH DAREDEVIL, PARACHUTES AT 13,000 FT. THEN *RIDES THE AIRWAVES* WITH A 4-FT. SURFBOARD STRAPPED TO HIS FEET.

IN *1876,* W.J. LEWIS OF NEW YORK CITY, INVENTED AN EARLY HELICOPTER THAT FLEW USING PROPELLERS *POWERED BY A HUGE SPRING* THAT RAN THE ENTIRE LENGTH OF THE MACHINE!

MOTOR-DRIVEN *ROLLER SKATES,* INVENTED BY ALPHONSE CONSTANTINI IN 1906, COULD TRAVEL *40 MILES AN HOUR!*

IN THE 1800s, CAPT. PAUL BOYTON OF N.J. — *WEARING AN INFLATABLE RUBBER TUNIC WITH A FLAG ATTACHED TO HIS TOE* — SAILED ACROSS THE ENGLISH CHANNEL AND DOWN THE *RHINE RIVER* AND DOWN THE *MISSISSIPPI.*

BELIEVE IT OR NOT! ANDRE GAMONET OF LYONS, FRANCE, INVENTED A SWIMMING DEVICE MADE OF *INFLATABLE RUBBER THAT FEATURED A HAND-OPERATED PROPELLER.*

IN AUG. 1990, TOM McCLEAN OF SCOTLAND CROSSED THE ATLANTIC OCEAN FROM NEW YORK TO ENGLAND IN 37 DAYS *IN A 37-FT-LONG STEEL JUG!*

AT THE RAGING WATERS THEME PARK in San Dimas, Ca., THE AUDIENCE AT A 'DRIVE-IN' THEATER **WATCHES MOVIES** *WHILE FLOATING ON INNER TUBES!*

BELIEVE IT OR NOT! FREDERIC BEAUCHÊNE AND THIERRY CARONI OF FRANCE SAILED 3200 MILES FROM NEW YORK TO ENGLAND IN 38 DAYS... *ON A 22-FOOT SAILBOARD!*

IN 1928, EXPLORER RICHARD HALLIBURTON SWAM THE *ENTIRE LENGTH* OF THE *50-MILE* PANAMA CANAL— AFTER REGISTERING HIMSELF AS A SHIP AND PAYING **36** CENTS IN TOLLS TO GET THROUGH THE CANAL'S *6 LOCKS!*

S.S. HALLIBURTON

AMERICAN *HELEN THAYER* SKIED 345 MILES FOR 27 DAYS ON A JOURNEY TO THE MAGNETIC NORTH POLE — *SURVIVING 7 ENCOUNTERS WITH POLAR BEARS, 3 BLIZZARDS AND NEAR-STARVATION.!*

THE FIRST HORSELESS CARRIAGE

SEEN IN CHATHAM, CANADA, BUILT BY WILLIAM MURRAY GRAY, IN 1905, WAS A WAGON POWERED BY A STEAM ENGINE FROM A BOAT-WHICH *HE CONVERTED TO GASOLINE*

WILLIAM CAVENDISH, A 19TH CENTURY BRITISH DUKE, HAD AN APARTMENT WITH AN *UNDERGROUND RAILROAD RUNNING FROM THE KITCHEN TO THE DINING ROOM!*

IN 1926 ROBERT H. GODDARD OF WORCHESTER, MA, THE FATHER OF ROCKET TECHNOLOGY, BUILT AND LAUNCHED A WORKING ROCKET WHICH ROSE 41 FEET INTO THE AIR AND LANDED 184 FEET FROM ITS LAUNCH PAD!

DON HELBIG OF CINCINNATI, OHIO, HAS TAKEN OVER 10,000 RIDES ON THE ROLLER-COASTER AT KINGS ISLAND AMUSEMENT PARK—A DISTANCE OF OVER 6,477 MILES.!

THE WORLD'S FIRST UFO LANDING PAD IS LOCATED IN THE REPUBLIC OF ST. PAUL, A TOWN IN ALBERTA, CANADA, THAT IS ALSO KNOWN AS *STARGATE ALPHA!*

SINCE 1977, JIM TERRION OF *PRINCE RUPERT, B.C.,* CANADA, HAS WALKED *39,905 MILES - WITHOUT LEAVING HIS HOME TOWN!*

HOGS WERE USED FOR NAVIGATION BY EARLY SAILORS WHO TOSSED THEM OVERBOARD IN THE BELIEF THEY WOULD *SWIM IN THE DIRECTION OF THE NEAREST LAND!*

A BUSINESSMAN IN *FINLAND*, WHO WAS CAUGHT SPEEDING ON A HIGHWAY NEAR *HELSINKI*, WAS *FINED* $13,400.

LARRY FUENTE OF MENDOCINO, CALIF., HAS DECORATED HIS CADILLAC WITH OVER **ONE MILLION PLASTIC DUCKS, BOWLING FIGURINES AND BEADS.**

BILL IRWIN, A BLIND HIKER FROM N. CAROLINA, WALKED THE 2,000-MILE-LONG APPALACHIAN TRAIL IN 8 MONTHS WITH ONLY HIS GUIDE DOG TO LEAD HIM!

WES WILLOUGHBY OF SAN FRANCISCO, CALIF., IS THE FIRST MAN IN HISTORY TO HAVE COLLECTED *CAR LICENSE PLATES* FROM *EVERY* JURISDICTION IN THE WORLD!

JONATHAN SCOBIE, AN AMERICAN BAPTIST MINISTER *INVENTED THE RICKSHAW* IN 1869 TO **CARRY HIS INVALID WIFE** THROUGH THE STREETS OF YOKOHAMA!

When Grover McIntyre of Chester, PA., died, he was buried in a custom made casket decorated with parts from his *MERCEDES-BENZ* car including the grille and hood ornament.

When Aurora Schuck of Aurora, IN, died in Nov., 1989, *HER BODY WAS BURIED INSIDE HER 1976 CADILLAC!*

*I*N THE 19ᵀᴴ CENTURY, TWO FRENCHMEN NAMED DE GRANDPRÉ AND LE PIQUE FOUGHT A DUEL WITH PISTOLS WHILE *RIDING IN HOT-AIR BALLOONS HALF A MILE ABOVE PARIS!*

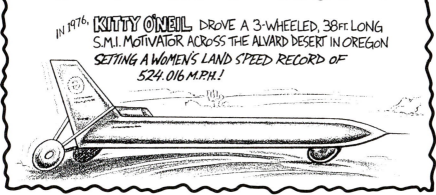

IN 1976, **KITTY O'NEIL** DROVE A 3-WHEELED, 38 FT. LONG S.M.I. MOTIVATOR ACROSS THE ALVARD DESERT IN OREGON *SETTING A WOMEN'S LAND SPEED RECORD OF 524.016 M.P.H.!*

A WOMAN IN NEW YORK CITY RECEIVED 2,800 *PARKING TICKETS* OVER A FOUR-YEAR PERIOD USING 36 *DIFFERENT* LICENSE PLATES--FOR A TOTAL FINE OF $171,746!

IN 1914, 4-YEAR-OLD **MAY PIERSTORFF** *WAS SHIPPED THROUGH THE U.S. MAIL* FROM HER HOME IN GRANGEVILLE, OH. TO HER GRANDMOTHER'S HOUSE--*100 MILES AWAY!*

A **SEATBELT FOR** *DOGS AND CATS* WAS INVENTED IN 1980 IN AUSTRIA!